trapdoor

To my good friend Elaine and her grandchildren,
Max, Evie, Hugo, Elliot and Hettie.

C F

For Loveday Super Spy!

R A

TOP TOP SECRET

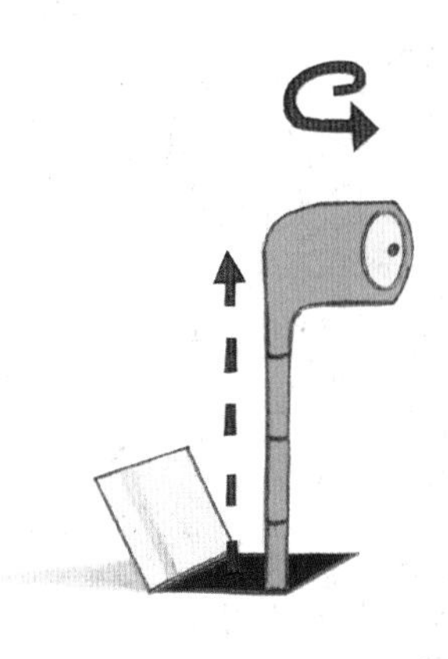

CLAIRE FREEDMAN
and RUSSELL AYTO

SIMON AND SCHUSTER
London New York Sydney Toronto New Delhi

It came in the middle of the
dark, dark night,
as silent as a spider
and tiptoe light.

The house lay in darkness,
and the streets asleep.
Only one boy heard it

Sid was awake, and do you know why?
Sid was a Secret agent Spy!

Under Sid's door slid a note which said:

Sid watched the note -

poooof -

self-ignite.

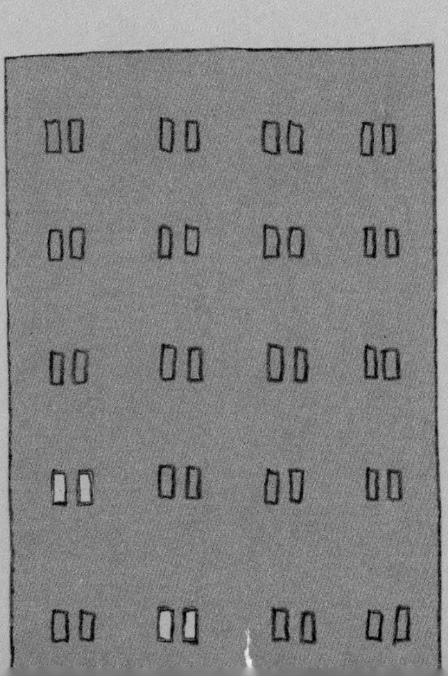

Then out he stole in the dark, dark night.

Close to the shadows, brave as a bear,

BOND J BOND
GADGETS AND GIZMOS

look left,

look right –

good, no one there.

Up steep steps,
down a long narrow lane,
left at the end
to an old empty drain.

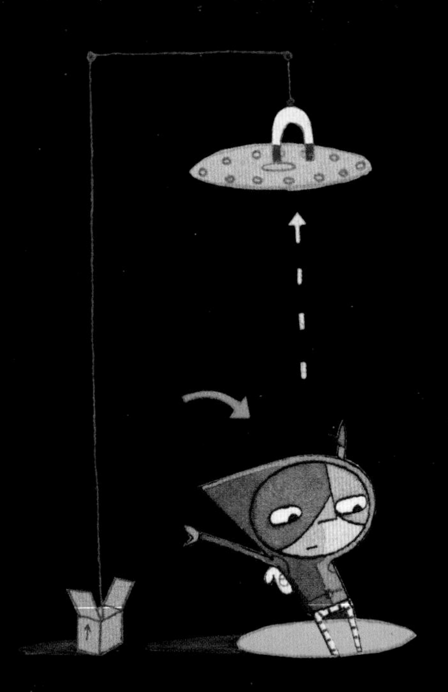

Sid clamped his magnet
to the big drain lid.

KER-LUNK!

It lifted and in Sid slid.

Quick as a
cockroach,

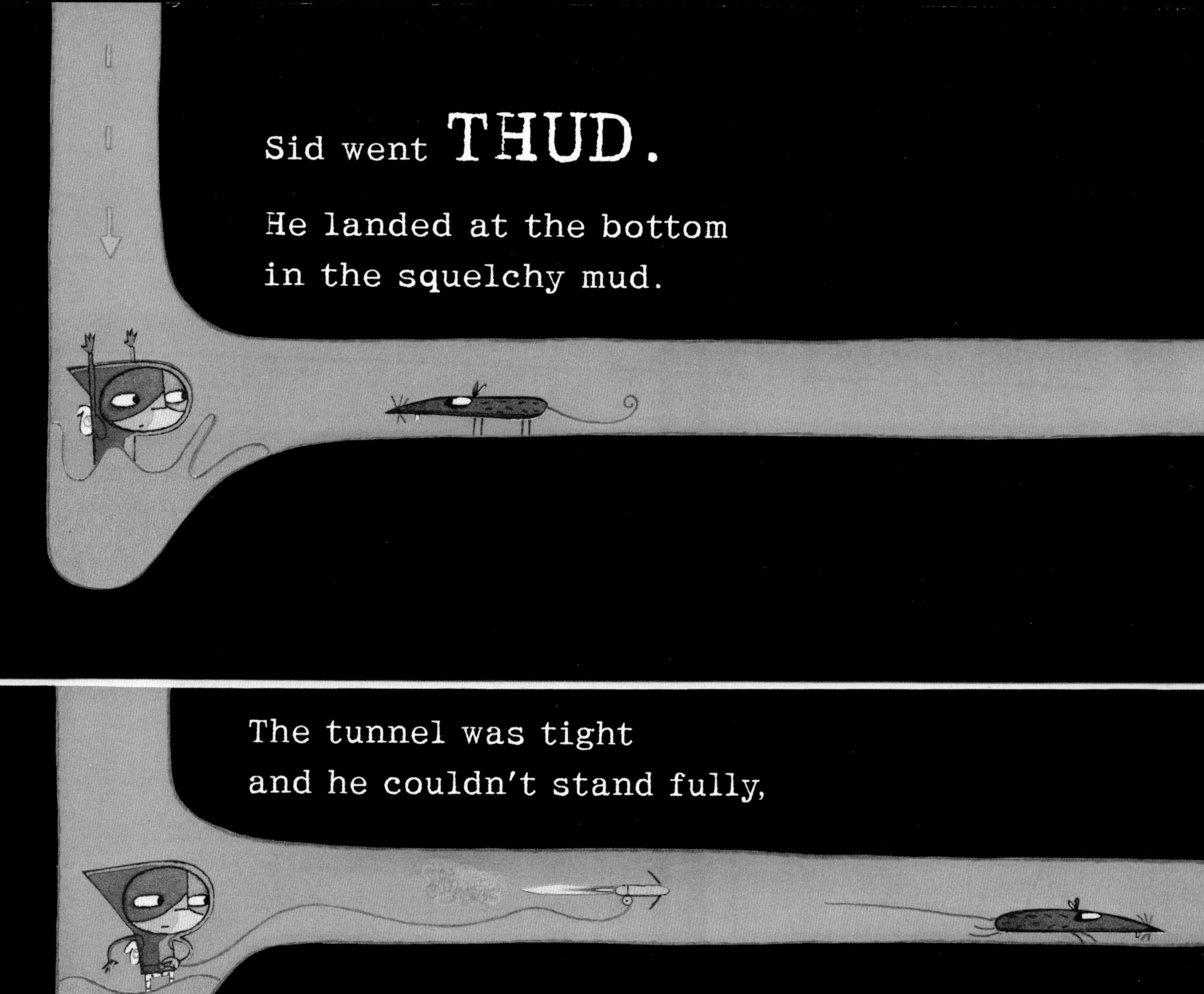

Sid went **THUD**.

He landed at the bottom
in the squelchy mud.

The tunnel was tight
and he couldn't stand fully,

so he hitched up a rope to his
supersonic pulley.

At the end was
the river -

Pull ring
to inflate

so he pumped up his raft.

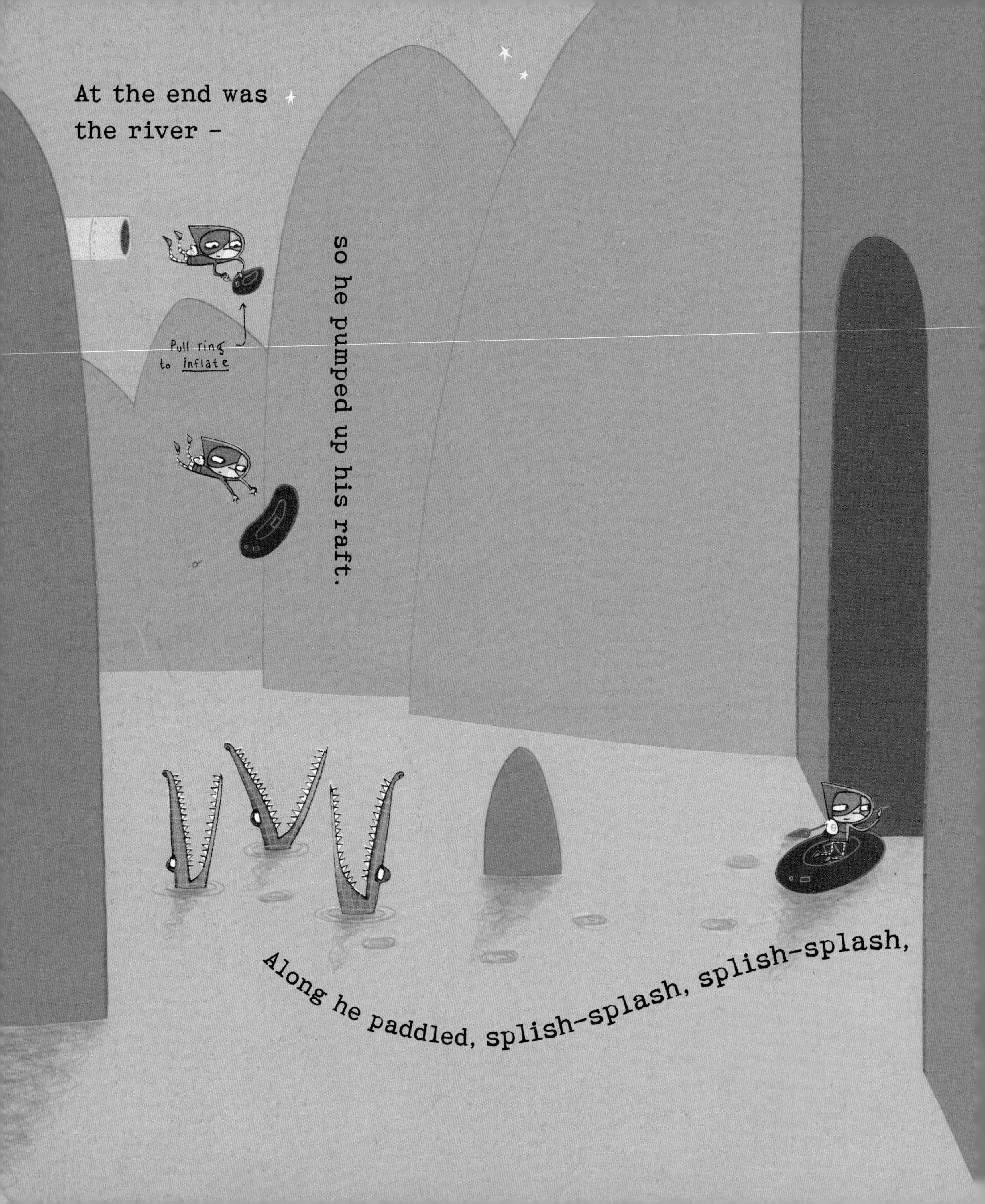

Along he paddled, splish-splash, splish-splash,

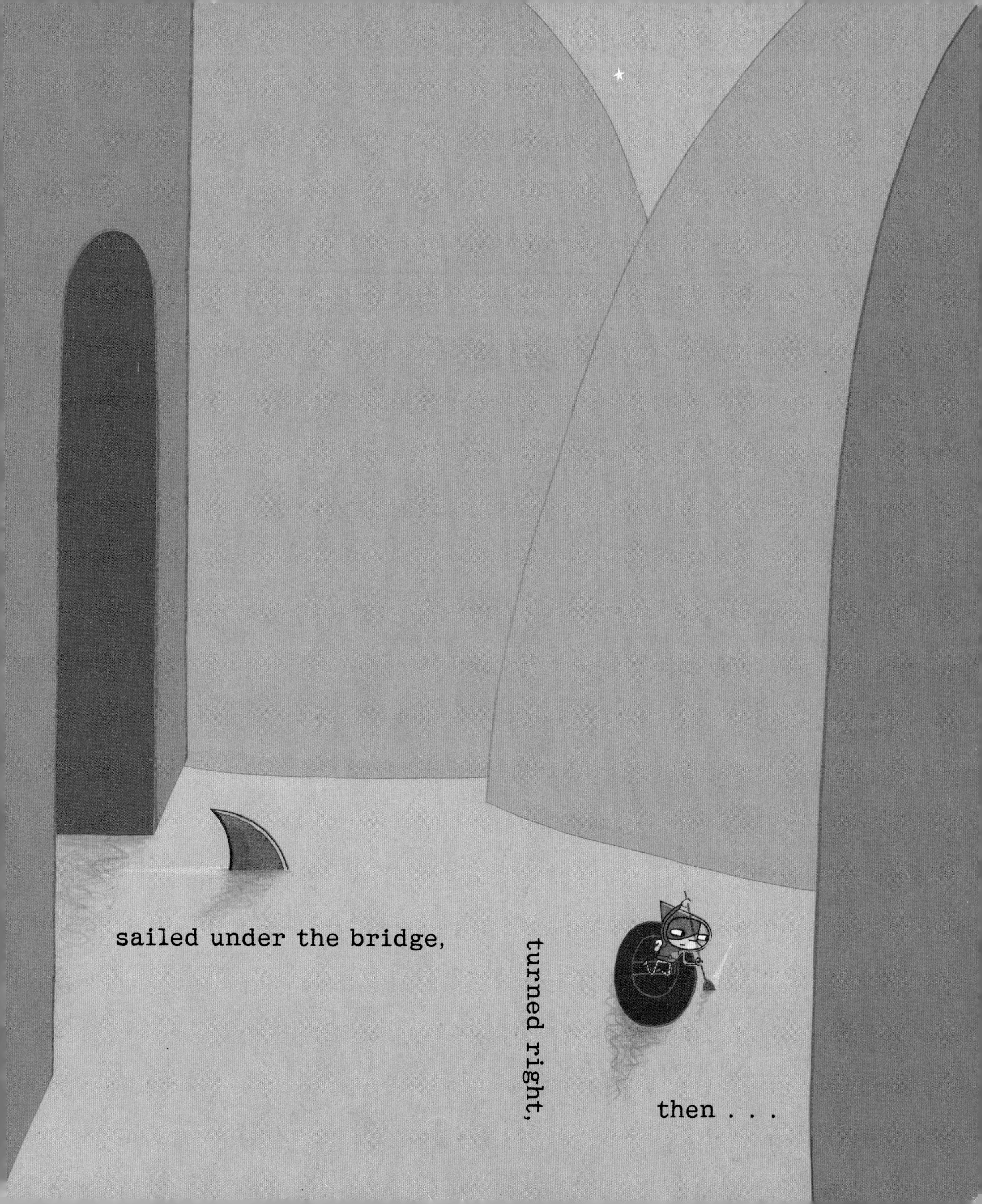
sailed under the bridge,
turned right,
then . . .

Sid clung fast to the green-slimed wall.
There was no way back - it was up or fall!

He squeezed from a tube some secret glue
and smeared his shoes with the gloopy goo.

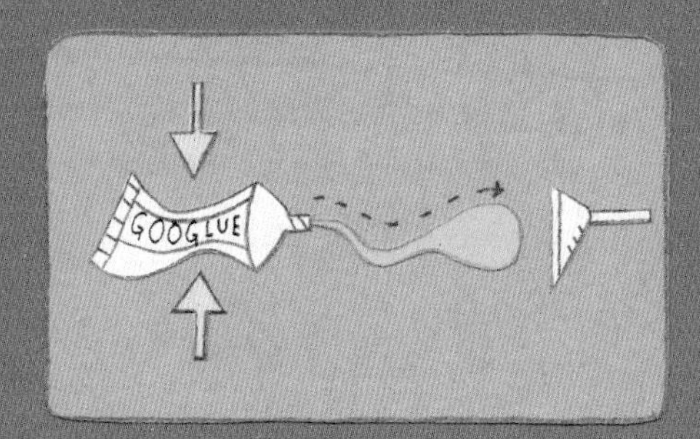

Up Sid walked, one step at a time.

Squelchy, squelch,

up the dripping slime.

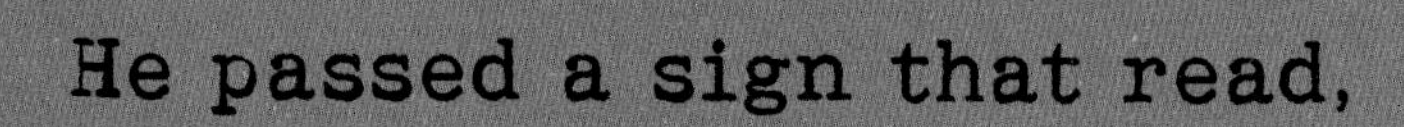

He passed a sign that read,

Beyond the walls of slippery slime,
The Dragon lived out his life of crime.

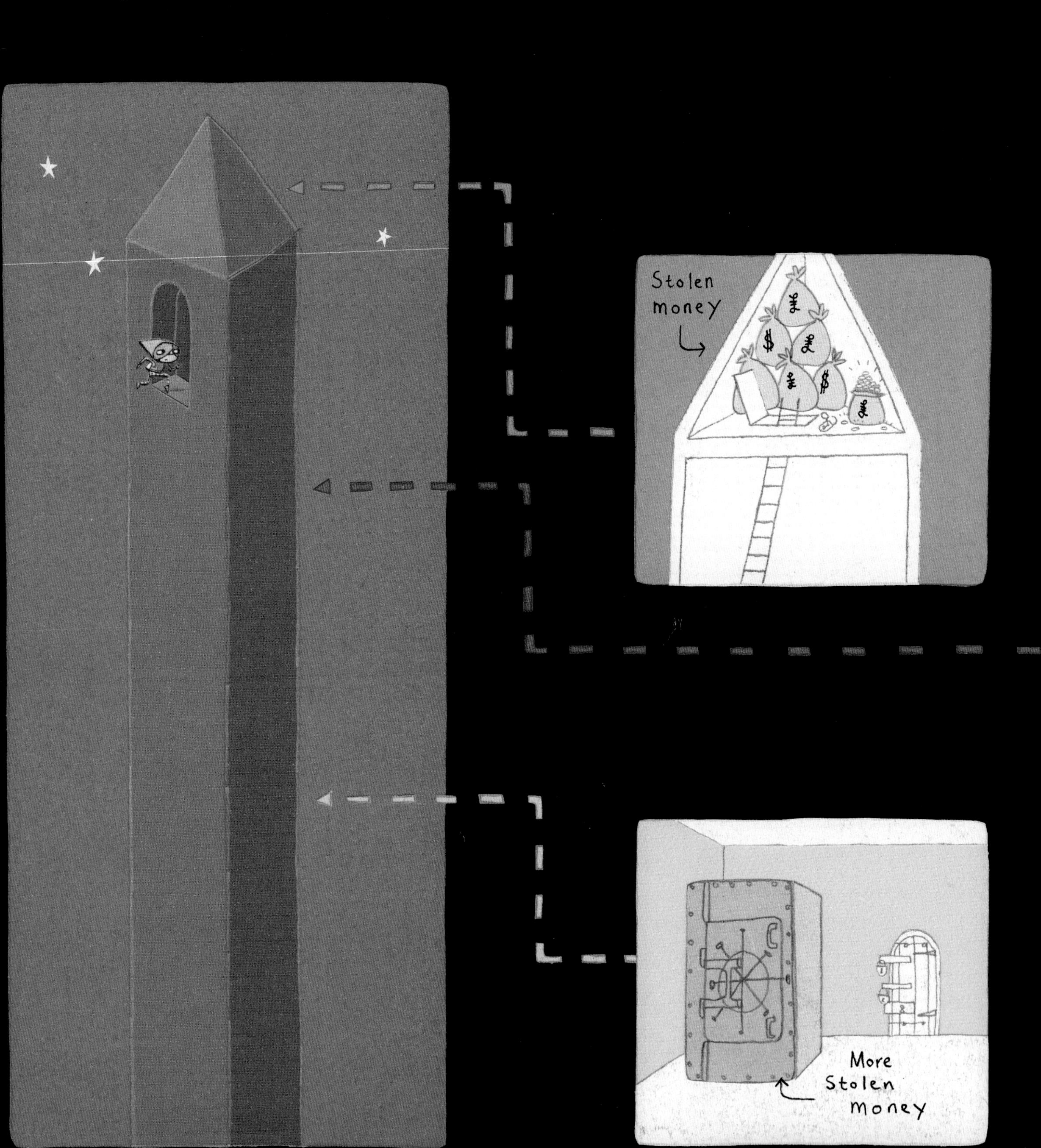

In through the window Sid soon crept.
And there, by the ring, The Dragon slept!

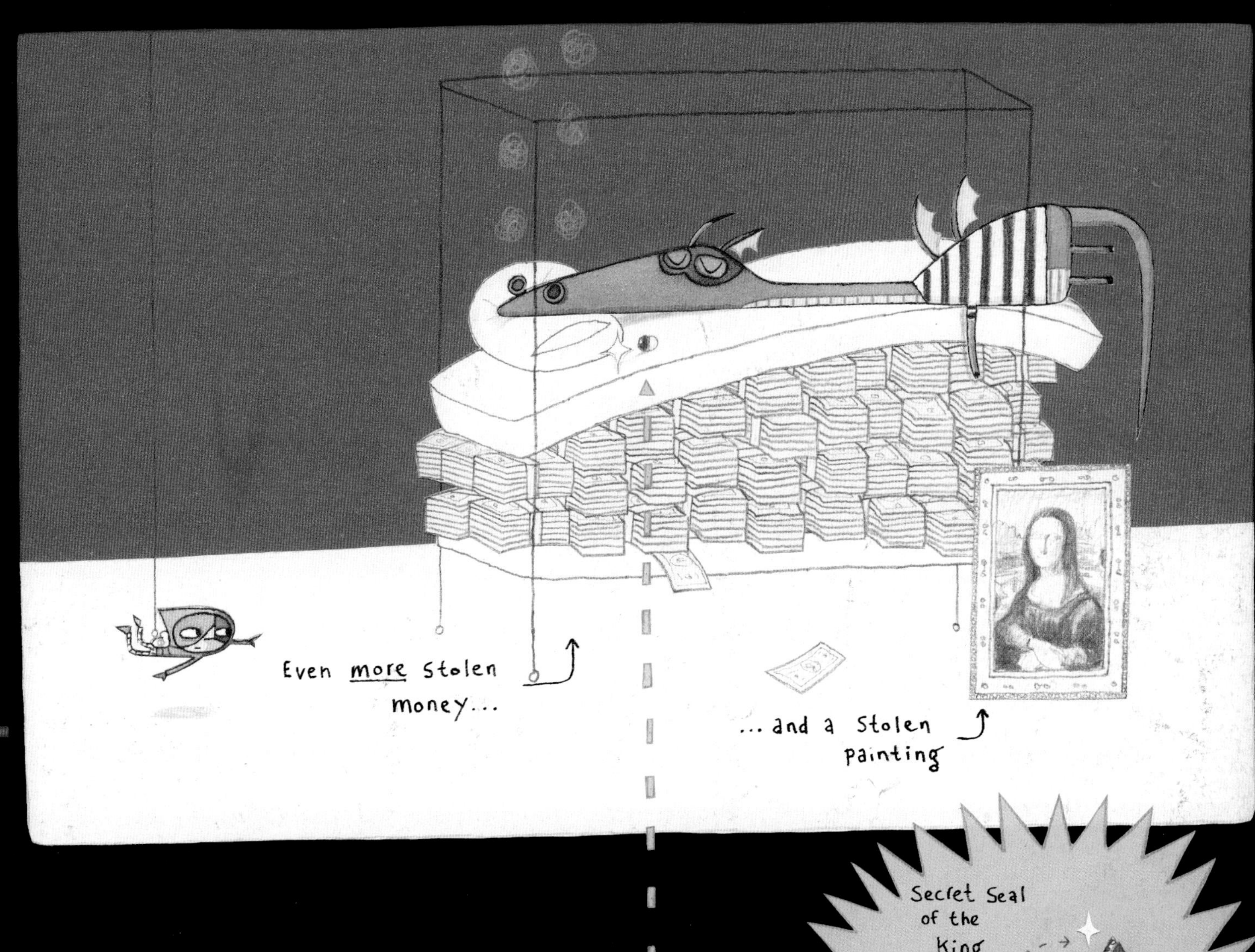

Stealing the gold
was the plan he'd laid.

Sid's mission?

To foil his evil raid.

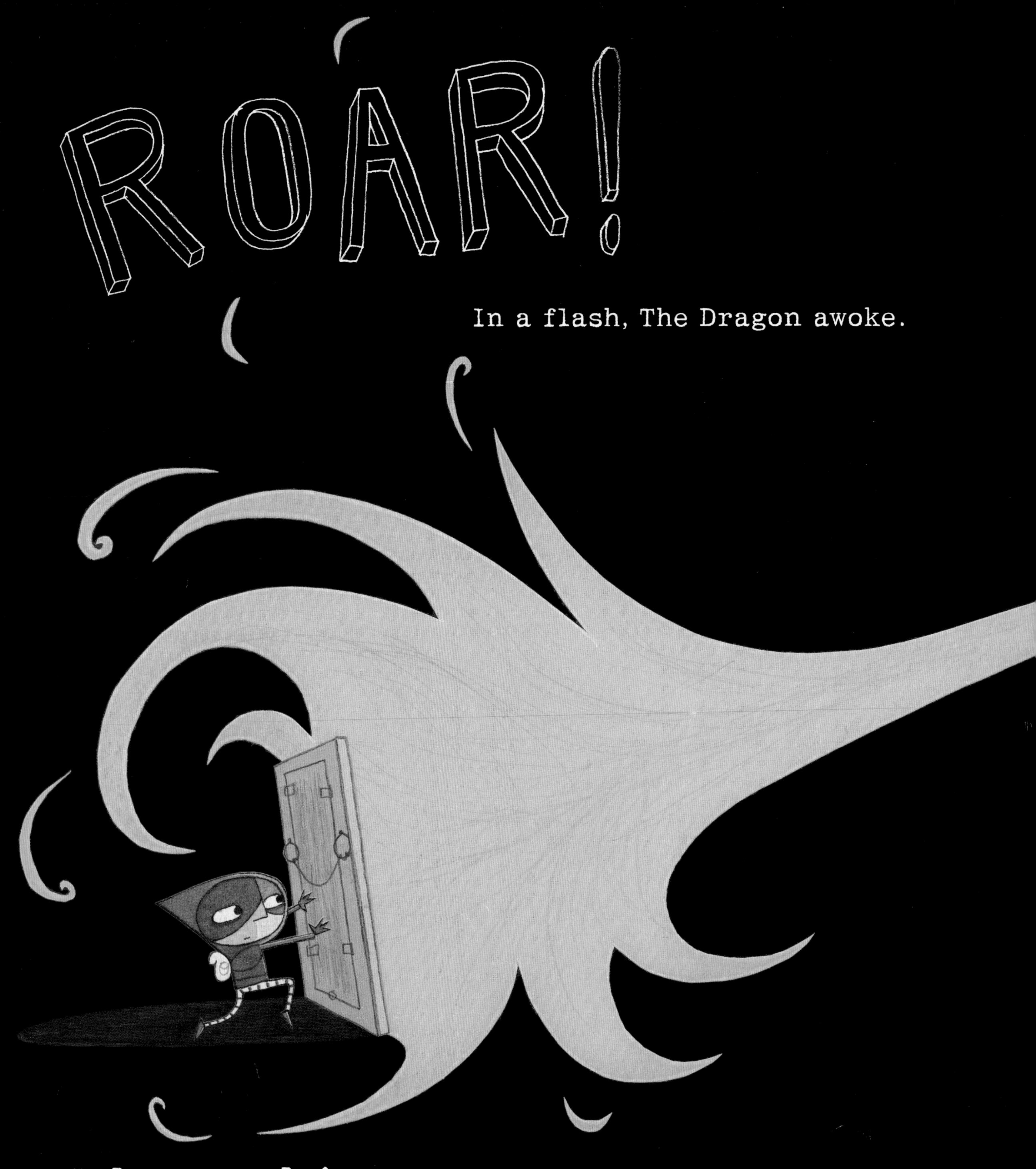

In a flash, The Dragon awoke.

Whoooosh! From his mouth burst flames and smoke

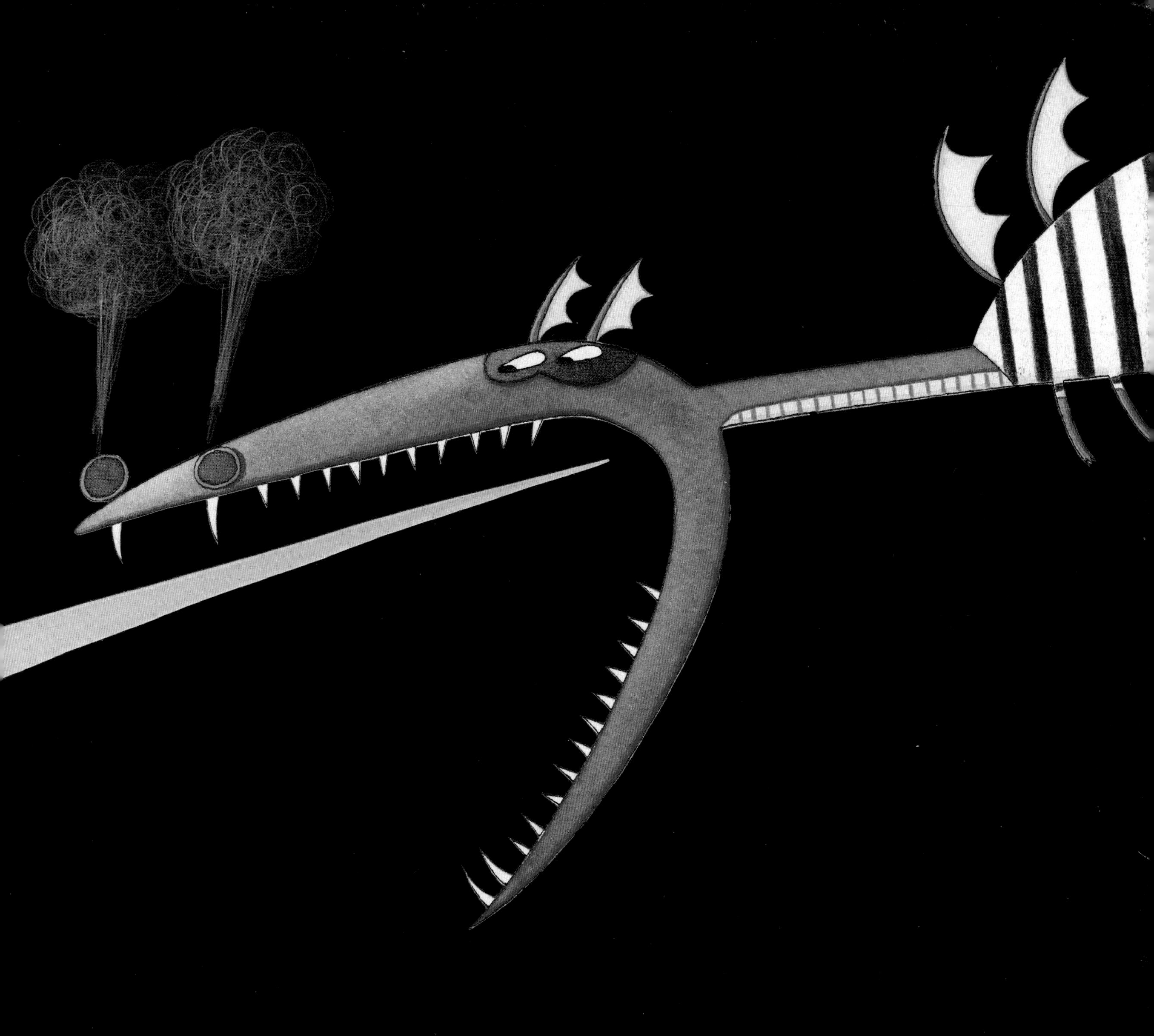

Sid reached down for his anti-dragon flare.

Oh no! It was lost! It wasn't there!

Even for Sid this
was somewhat tricky.

Could he use something else?
Something nice and sticky?

A very old toffee,
all covered in fluff . . .
Was it enough to quench
The Dragon's puff?

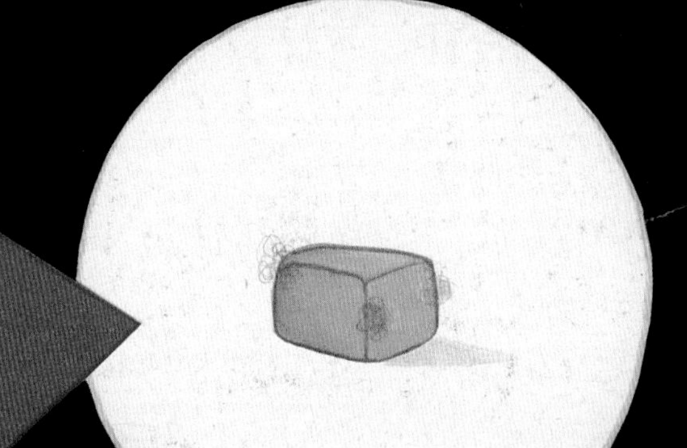

RAAAAR!

roared The Dragon

and leapt to his feet.

Sid quickly threw him the toffee to eat.

The super-sticky toffee soon clamped shut his jaws.

He couldn't breathe fire.

There were no more **roars.**

Sid snatched the ring - held it in his teeth.

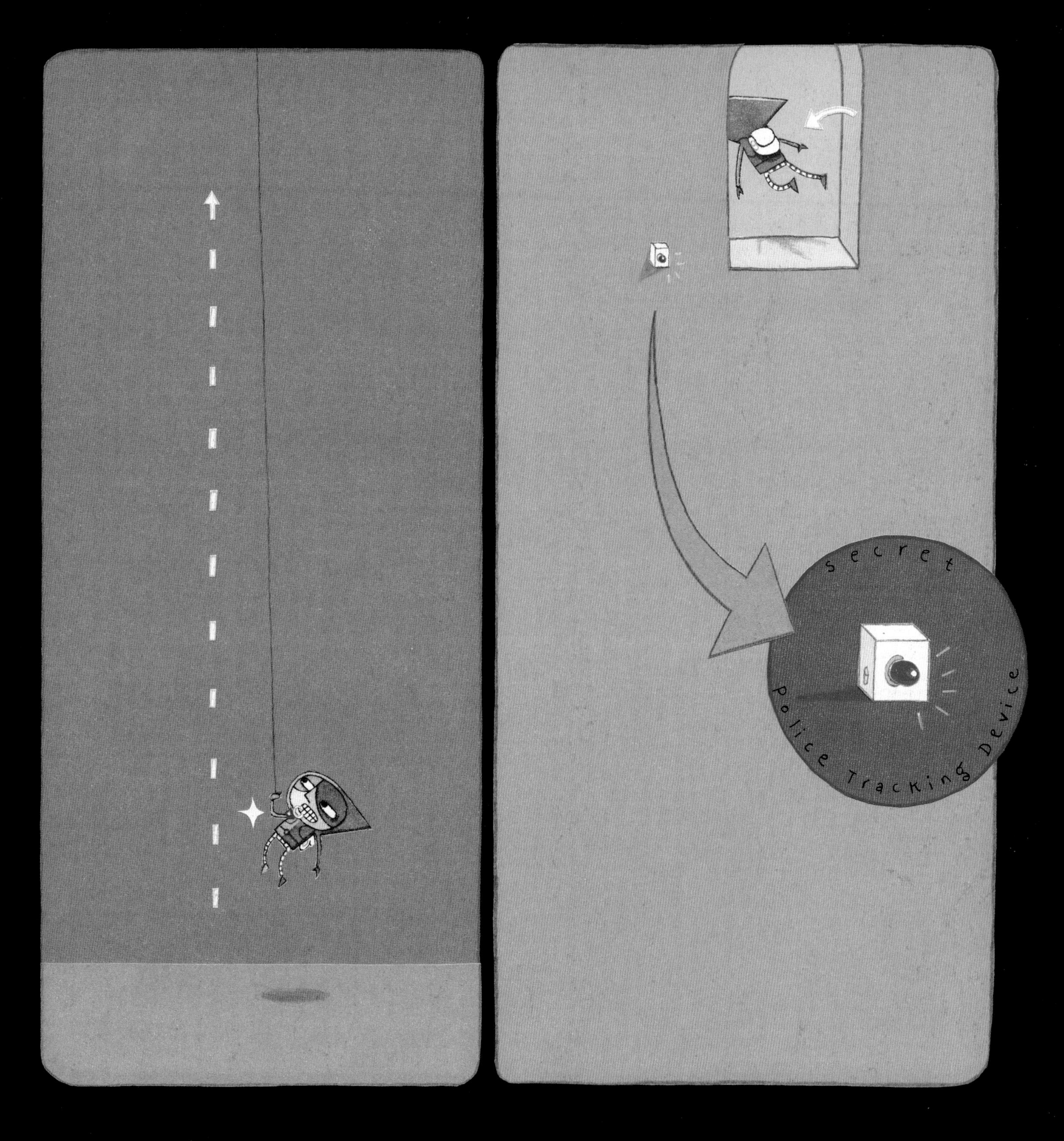

Then jumped out the window in great relief.

Down, down the wall, all covered in slime . . .

He reached the bottom in the nick of time!
Clipped on his go-fast, telescopic skis
and skimmed through the water with super-charged ease.

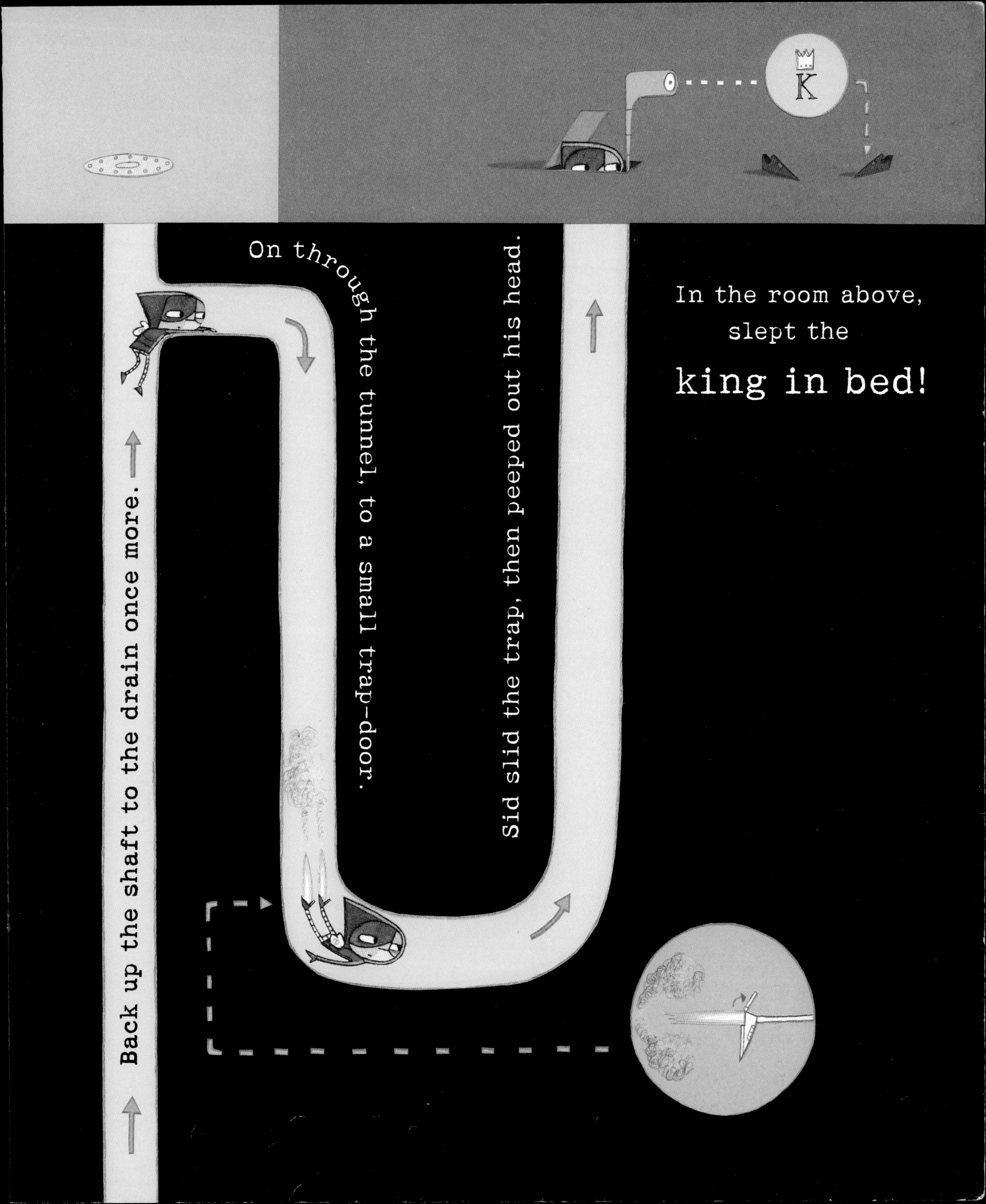
Back up the shaft to the drain once more.
On through the tunnel, to a small trap-door.
Sid slid the trap, then peeped out his head.
In the room above, slept the
king in bed!
K

Sid tripped up and over he rolled.

OH NO! The ring bounced from his hold.

he shot out his hand but it spun down a crack!

HELP!

Out came the magnet . . .

PHEW! Got it back.

Slowly, slowly,
don't drop the ring.

Back in the jewel box,
back with the king.

Sid wiped his brow. **Hooray** – job done!
A tough, tough mission, but brilliant fun.

Back to his bed our hero crept.
Soon Sid the secret agent slept.

Two hours later, the king cried,

And only we know how!